The Call for *Emily*

Samantha C. Sinclair

ISBN 979-8-89243-242-9 (paperback)
ISBN 979-8-89243-243-6 (digital)

Christian Faith Publishing
832 Park Avenue
Meadville, PA 16335
www.christianfaithpublishing.com

Printed in the United States of America

This book is in loving memory of Tony King, who made a good lasting impact on my life, and many others.

This book is dedicated to the following people with love:

Tasha

Trish

Lars

Nissy

Charles

Heather

Isaiah

Richard

Chris

Kristy

Ron

Filamay

The LORD is my shepherd; I shall not want. He maketh me to lie down in green pastures: he leadeth me beside the still waters. He restoreth my soul: he leadeth me in the paths of righteousness for his name's sake. Yea, though I walk through the valley of the shadow of death, I will fear no evil: for thou art with me; thy rod and thy staff they comfort me. Thou preparest a table before me in the presence of mine enemies: thou anointest my head with oil; my cup runneth over. Surely goodness and mercy shall follow me all the days of my life: and I will dwell in the house of the LORD forever.

—Psalm 23:1–6 KJV

Note from the Author

God is the true author, without *Him*, none of this would be possible.

This is a work of fiction. Any reference to any person or situation is truly coincidental. Although I'm basing this book in a real location, I have taken liberty with towns and locations. You may find some locations mentioned in their truth.

November Thursday afternoon

It was a dark and stormy evening. Myself and Susann had been on the job for just over twenty hours. That isn't a typical shift for a 911 telecommunicator. However, I had already been stuck on a sixteen-hour shift because I had to cover for a coworker. Now, the road to the dispatch center was covered in snow and probably ice. Why somebody had thought it a good idea to put dispatch and EMS on Community Hill, the steepest hill in Sevierville, I'll never know.

Now, not only were myself and Susann stuck, but so were the three crews who served the county upstairs.

"This is just wonderful." Susann slapped her desk. "My daughter is stuck with an eighteen-year-old sitter who only knows how to cook ramen noodles. At least there is soup in the cabinet. I know, I know, we have bigger issues."

"Well"—I calmly eased a cup of hot strong black coffee onto my desk—"your daughter eating is an issue, so I'm glad there is soup. Yes, it is an issue when all three ambulances and crews are stuck in the building. Even the parking lot is a solid sheet of ice." I happened to know because I went to my car for my charger. The one in the radio room quit about an hour ago. I had nearly busted my tail on the quick errand.

We heated up some supper and settled in for what looked a lengthy stay. Around 6:00 p.m., just as we were making a plan for splitting naps and radio/phone time, movement on the camera monitoring on the outside the building caught both our attention.

"What is that?" I blurted first.

"I don't know, but it definitely isn't a dog."

Just then, we heard the bell, indicating the front door was opened.

Who would be? Before I could finish my thought of who would be out now, we heard the front door slamming shut and the cry of a baby. I leaped out of my chair, along with Susann, who was ten steps ahead of me.

I rushed to the baby, and she raced outside to try and get a glimpse of the parent or whoever had dropped the baby here. *How did they get up that hill?* Well, however they had, I was glad they brought her there. It was a little girl who didn't look to be more than a newborn. I took her and her pink rabbit blanket in my arms, just as Susann came back in shivering.

"Did you gain anything?"

"Just saw some kid running, then sliding down Community Hill. How's the baby?"

"Let's have upstairs come and take a look at her. She definitely isn't going anywhere. I don't know how they got up this hill."

While she called upstairs, I snuggled the little girl to me and sang softly. It was odd to me how it still came natural, seeing as how I hadn't been around many children for years. I put in a call to the deputy on call who wasn't tied up and let him know what was going on, not that he could get up here.

Five minutes later, Laura Thompson and her EMS partner, Jason Homes, came down the steps and entered into the radio room. Jason, an EMT of five years, stood about five foot eight. He had light-brown hair and bright-blue eyes. He also had a thick New York accent to go with it. Laura, a medic of ten years, had long dark hair and a thin build. She stood about five feet. Laura had a six-week-old baby at home, and this was just her second shift back. She instantly took and checked the baby over.

"She looks healthy, and breath sounds are good. She's not very old."

"How old do you think she is?" I rolled my chair close to Laura's.

"I'd say a few hours old." Laura snuggled the baby and said, "Makes me miss mine. I really thought about quitting several times, but I came back."

"What are we going to do with her?" Susann asked.

"You all can't get her down the hill safely."

"That's for sure," Susann chimed in. "Knox County is covering for you all because you can't get down the hill."

"Don't we know it?" Homes and Laura groaned.

"We need a new building and a new location," Laura muttered under her breath.

"Pretty sad we are here, and can't respond to anything," Jason added.

Jason picked up a cookie from the table. That was one thing about Thanksgiving, every church and business seemed to bring on the meals, and we were grateful.

"Well"—Laura smiled—"I think I know why God put me here now."

She handed me the baby and left the room. She popped her head in and said, "I'll be right back. I have something for the baby. We need it now."

I was wondering what we were going to feed the baby, and the only diaper was the one she wore. Within minutes, I was reminded for the second time that day just how much we should trust *God* because *He* always provides what we need. I smiled as Laura reentered the room.

Chapter 1

Ten weeks had gone by since that day in the radio room. I had spent Christmas with my thirty-year-old daughter, Alexandria. She wasn't keen on my idea, but it was happening.

Neither was my sister Sharon. She wasn't keen on much of anything. Sharon Lyn (we just called her Sharry) was thirteen years my senior. We were daylight and dark. Sharry now had salt and pepper hair. Mine was still that tint of red it'd always been, and my blue eyes stood out. She liked to have things her way, and it's her way or the highway. Sherry had become more of a homebody, "leave me be," so I did.

My daughter, Alex, said I was too old to start over, but I knew that she was jealous. Although she had moved out and into a college dorm the day she turned eighteen and was married by twenty-five, she'd still been an only child since she was born.

I was eighteen when she was born, married to, and pregnant with, a man's child, who I thought I loved. Honestly, I don't have any idea what I saw in him. But that's me, see-the-some-good-in-every-body woman, and I was lonely. I made myself a promise and kept it: my kids, they'd never ever experience what I did. But anyway, that's for later. Just for the record, I am certainly not too old to start over. I am forty-eight years old and spry as any twenty-eight-year-old. If I want to raise Emily, and *God* works it out, I will, and *He* has.

Chapter 2

Now, I am not a particularly noisy person; in fact, I think it is down-right unfriendly to be so. But when you walk into a conversation or scene that you just can't leave, sometimes by choice, that's another story. That's what happened to me on this particular sunny day.

Our bathroom happened to be in progress of being worked on down in the basement at dispatch, so if Susann or myself needed to make a run, we had to do it up those stairs. Well, to say the least, it was inconvenient. On one of these trips, I was headed back minding my own business, and as I rounded the stairwell corner, I heard and saw something that made me stop in my tracks. I could not believe these two would do any such. I was around that corner before I knew what hit me and saw Laura in Jason's arms. She was crying, and I just had noticed that part of it. I took ten knots backward and cleared my throat.

"Excuse me." I cleared my throat again apologetically. "I'm sorry I—"

"You weren't interrupting anything."

"It isn't what it looks like." Laura's face reddened more than it was from crying. "My babies' dad just told me he left. He left our daughter with his mother, and my mother is on her way to pick her up. He's in love with another woman." She finished falling apart, in Jason's arms.

You definitely become family in emergency services, and I need to learn to not assume things before I get all the info to CAD it in my brain. Well, I hugged Laura and raced back downstairs. Who knew if the county was going wild? It was a warm day. No sooner had I gotten downstairs and back in my chair than I got the call I'd been waiting for. My home was approved, and I could adopt Emily Rose.

The process was complete. Despite what my daughter, her husband, and my sister, Sharon, said, Emily Rose was my daughter, sent from *God* above. The first night home was anything but easy. I got her home around five and was settling her in to her new crib, swing, and my arms. That was the plan anyway. I noticed white spots on Emily's arms and legs, and I could tell her eyes weren't acting like other babies her age. She didn't look at me, at least not with her right eye. I planned to point out these things to her pediatrician the next morning. About 10:00 p.m., I was putting her down. She had taken her bottle and burped for me, and I had bathed her. It felt good. If I didn't have any support from my family, I had plenty from my coworkers, my work family. That's what we are, a family.

As I laid her down, Emily started to jerk. I figured she might be about to cry, protesting being put down despite being asleep. But things went south. It wasn't a midnight cry for holding or for a bottle. She was seizing, and all I could do, other than prayer, was put out the call for Emily, my new baby. It's a strange feeling really, being on the opposite end of the line, giving Jill the address, and listening to her page medical, for my baby girl.

Although I'd only had Emily in my home for a few hours, I felt as if she had come right out of my own womb. I had been carrying her in my heart and hadn't even known it. I had no idea I even needed this little girl or she needed me, and now, I might lose her before we even got started? All I could pray as I climbed into the ambulance, and Laura worked on her as Jason sped along, was, "God, please don't take my baby!"

There was no history of seizures, they had checked the chart, and the social worker asked the foster parents for any information. They had noticed her eyesight but hadn't yet mentioned it to the doctor. The white spots came out of nowhere. They did a full CT scan on Emily, and the findings were horrific.

A couple of hours later, my older daughter showed up with her husband right behind her. "Mom, I'm sorry." She put her slender arms around me, with the scent of her strawberry shampoo mixed with the smell of the hospital. That hug—it felt so good. "I was wrong. I see how happy Emily, Sissy, makes you, and I can't believe this is happening to her."

"Me either, honey. Me either. You're here now, and that's all that matters. It's forgiven." Not that Alex needed forgiveness for anything, but I knew she needed to hear it—a mother just knows.

"I'm sorry, Mrs. Pennacheck."

"When will you ever start calling me Versie? I am your mother-in-law, not your first-grade teacher. Thank you two for coming and having that change of heart."

"Of course, Momma. I was pretty selfish. We need her, and she needs us."

Alexandria was becoming a nurse, and her husband, Brad, was in law school. I was proud of them both. Now, if my sister could just come around. It was about that time they returned with Emily and laid her in my arms. They had to put her out for the CT scan, so she was resting for the moment. The seizure had lasted for ten minutes, and it had taken her little body a while to come out of it. It was just then that her little body began to convulse again. Brad, my daughter's husband, left the room. Alex, however, calmly took the baby girl and laid her on the bed. The monitors began to go off, and my daughter stopped breathing. What happened over the next half hour is a miracle. They did CPR on Emily and put in a breathing tube. She was admitted to the hospital, and by the next morning, thank *God*, was able to breathe on her own. My daughter stayed with us that night, my first night with both my girls, but not how I pictured it.

The next morning, the doctor came in, shut the door, and sat down. "We need to talk," she said, looking at the other three doctors who had followed her into the room.

I braced for anything and prayed harder if that were possible. I wanted to hit my knees, but like when I was on a stressful 911 call, I had to stay in my chair. I put my hands on my knees and opened my eyes wider to keep from closing them. I couldn't shut this out no matter how bad I wanted to. This was my baby girl. My daughter seemed to see the need for supporting me and braced me by putting a gentle arm around my neck.

"Mrs. Pennacheck—"

"Please," I said, "call me Versie."

"Versie," the doctor lifted her eyes to mine, "your daughter has a tumor on her brain. Also, there is one in her right eye. The white spots on the skin are an indicator of something that goes along with the seizures and tumors. We will need to biopsy them if we notice any growth. However, it is unlikely they are cancerous."

"What are you saying, doctor?" I knew there was more.

"We are diagnosing your daughter with TSC."

What in the world were they talking about? My daughter did not have anything. What even is TSC? Tuberous sclerosis complex—that was Emily's diagnosis. There was more the doctor had to say. She also had a tumor in her right kidney. We would start medication, to try to shrink them when the doctor felt comfortable doing that. Also, the doctor said that they would need to perform a specialized test on Emily to see where all the white spots showed up. That would come later. The test would only work in a completely darkened room.

Over the next few weeks and months, they performed tests on my daughter and tried to find a seizure medication that would work. Thankfully, my daughter and her husband had an extra bedroom. Emily and I stayed with them a lot. I was often exhausted trying to care for her on my own and needed support. Sometimes, when we were off the next day, my friend and coworker, Susann, along with her daughter, would come spend the night with Emily and I at our house. That was helpful. My sister, Sharon, however, was not helpful in the least. The only thing she liked to do was call and bad-mouth me and my baby.

"If people would take care of their own," she mouthed, "you wouldn't be in this predicament. You are too old and single. Alexandrea has her own life, and that coworker of yours has hers too. Get over yourself, and do the right thing."

"Which is?" I said, getting ready to put the phone down.

"Get rid of that problem child."

She would have gone on, except for the fact I told her to not call me unless she had a change of heart about Emily and it was Alex's choice to be in mine and the baby's life. She didn't call back that day, and I didn't know if she would. My sister has her own life and ways; that's it. I love her, but I'm not so sure she does me. If you don't love my kids, you don't love me.

The appointment didn't show many more white spots than we could already see on her skin. Six months into it, her seizure medicine was helping. Emily was still suffering through around five severe seizures a week and light ones in between.

On her first birthday, we had an appointment with Emily's doctor. She declared the medicine, phenobarbital, a current success. Her seizures had slowed, although she was still suffering from several a week.

"What do you mean by current success?" I asked.

"Well," she took Emily's small hand, "unfortunately, the medication can stop working at any point. The likelihood is that we will have to change medication several times. How is OT and physical therapy going?"

Emily was receiving several kinds of therapy. She had severe delays. At age one, she was not crawling and talking nor able to eat solid foods. She was diagnosed with Down syndrome and autism spectrum disorder. I wondered if my baby would ever walk, talk, or do anything on her own. My sister called again one day soon after she was diagnosed with this at age nine months. On top of the TSC, this was a lot to process.

"Versie Gail," she snapped, "will that baby ever be able to do anything productive? Maybe you should just let them keep her comfortable until she dies."

I could not believe what I was hearing. I slammed the phone down in her ear, but not before saying this, "My daughter is already doing something productive. Jesus has a reason for putting her on this earth and in my arms. You have never even met her."

"And Alex has stopped talking to me because of her."

At that point was when I put the phone down, in a rough manner.

Her first birthday was in mermaids. I let Alex pick out the theme. We wondered if she would ever be able to carry a child. She and my son-in-law had already suffered five miscarriages. My daughters were inseparable now. She and Brad were loving the three nights a week they got to babysit while I worked. I actually worked days, but since I went in early, they insisted Emily spend the night. Sometimes, I did too.

Anyway, her first birthday was marked by smiles and giggles. Emily even laughed out loud once, and that was the first time. She couldn't have cake; however, we let her lick the icing. Doctors had put in a feeding tube at five months due to her severe issues with swallowing. However, she had passed her swallowing test at eleven months and could handle certain liquids. We were slowly trying to introduce soft things. But still, unless it was something liquid or pudding, she couldn't tolerate swallowing it. She choked on me a few times. I prayed this would improve.

Our church family came, my family, and my coworkers. Laura and Jason were there, together, with Laura's daughter. Her husband had divorced her and left her and their baby girl without a word almost a year ago. She and Jason hadn't announced anything officially yet, but we all knew.

My sister, Sharon, came prancing through the door; yeah, she got invited. I thought if she saw Emily, she'd fall in love with her and change her heart. But no, that isn't what happened.

"You are really having a party and celebrating what? All these people are wasting their time, and so are you."

"Get out, Sharon." I held my breath for ten seconds as I held the door open. She snapped something about being invited as she pressed out the door. "Why'd you come?" I called after her. "If it was such a waste of your time? My daughter is not a waste of anyone's time. Don't call me again. I'll keep praying for you. I love you, Shar."

I was exhausted by the end of the day, but Emily was smiling, and that meant everything to me. Emily smiled a lot, and I tried to take lessons.

We got ready for bed that night, and my cell phone rang. It was Laura Ann.

"Hello," I said, quietly putting Emily in bed next to me.

"Did I wake you?"

"No, I'm not asleep just yet. Emily is though. She's exhausted."

"I would say so. She was passed around fifty times."

"I know. I just hope she didn't pick anything up. But she had an awesome time."

"We did too, nice party. Save any decorations you have. I can use them for Trinity Louann. By the way, Jason and I have something to tell you. We are officially dating. Trinity thinks he is her daddy."

"That's all she has ever known." I squeezed in a word.

"Yes, well," she laughed, "don't go picking out your bridesmaid dress just yet. It's gonna be a while. We're taking it slow."

"That's a good thing to do. I'm happy for you all, and I'll be praying."

"Thanks. Yeah, Trinity's dad hasn't had any contact with her for six months. I'm talking to a lawyer Monday about pulling his rights."

"Can you do that?"

"I don't know. We shall have to see." She sounded tired, physically and mentally. My heart broke for her.

"Well, keep me posted. Hey, Laura, Em is having a seizure. I got to go."

"Is she okay?"

"I'll leave the phone on speaker. Dear *God*, help us. She's turning blue around her mouth and nose." My mind went blank. "Dear God," I broke down, "what do I do?"

"Call 911, and I'll be right over."

Once again, my little girl was raced to the hospital. Once again, my daughter and her husband were on hand for support. Not far behind them were Jason and Laura; Laura's mother kept Trinity. Emily was placed on life support and flown to Children's North fifty miles south of here. I wanted to fly with her, but I was a basket case. I passed out on the floor in the lobby.

I came to in a bed, and all I knew was I had to get to my daughter. Alexandrea stood over me with a worried look on her face.

"Where's your sister?" were the first words out of my mouth.

"In the air with Laura."

Dear sweet Laura, of course, she would fly with Emily. I would have to thank her later. For now, I had to get out of here. I had to get to my daughter. First I had to relax so that my blood pressure would go down. That was hard to do. I took some slow deep breaths, allowing myself to breathe out longer than in. I closed my eyes and imagined myself running into the arms of Jesus. In a couple of hours, Alex and I were on the road.

Once we hit the interstate and it was getting daylight by this point, I called our pastor. He graciously agreed to put her on the phone prayer chain and have a special prayer for Emily and our family once the church gathered later that morning.

Alex drove the speed limit, although I could tell she wanted to break it. I reminded her that we needed to get there in one piece to be any good to Emily. We arrived within driving time and were led to Emily's side. She was stable, but still not breathing on her own, at least, not completely. The doctor came immediately to our side and ushered us into his office.

"I'm afraid what I have isn't good."

"Has the seizure done more damage to my sister?" Alex asked in a confident tone.

"Well," he cleared his throat and looked us straight in the eye, "it's more than that this time I'm afraid."

How could it possibly be more?

"I'm sorry," I grabbed my head, "what?"

"I know," he said, placing his hand palm down on the desk. "But unfortunately, your daughter has suffered a stroke."

What in the world was he talking about our Emily?

"Dear God, wasn't TSC enough? Did she have to have a stroke too?" I wanted to be angry, but I just couldn't because I knew my little one was in the best hands possible, no matter what happened.

For days, my baby stayed like that, her body trying to recover. A stroke in a child—I asked Alex about it. She said it does happen, sometimes before they are born. Doesn't this show people they are live humans, even in the womb?

On day five, she was finally able to come off life support all the way. My aunt had called and sent me some money, and my sister called too, but it wasn't for encouragement. It was to put me down for continuing this precious baby's life. Laura and Jason made the drive to check on us, and on day three, Alex had to get home for nursing school; she also held down a job.

But on day five, Emily showed everyone just what *God* does. She opened her eyes wider than she had in days and smiled that pretty smile. She reached out her arms for me but had no movement in her right leg. Her right arm was a little weak, but they planned to begin therapy as soon as possible. It wasn't until they did a test on her eyes that we knew for sure, but it appeared she now had little-to-no sight in her right eye.

Over the next couple of years, the baby continued to experience seizures. It had dropped to three severe a week now, with mild seizures in between.

Chapter 3

Over the next three years, more would happen than I could dream. EMS got their new building, so I saw less of Jason and Laura. They wed in the fall. I couldn't be happier for them.

Emily did get her sight back slowly, and movement in her right leg was slim; her arm was stiff all the time. She could not move it. Alex grew closer to Emily and took a class on physical therapy, as it would be a help to her in nursing as well. She and Brad also learned, and shared the news, that they were expecting.

Tragically, their happiness was short-lived, as Alex miscarried at twenty weeks. They already had plenty of stuff for the baby, and the nursery was halfway set up. Alex shied away from her favorite floor for weeks, labor and delivery.

"Too painful." She cried on the phone to me one night. She was working down in the emergency department one night, and a baby was born there. She said that reminded her of *God's* true miracle of life and that her babies were safe in heaven. She willingly took her rotation that week. It was still hard for her, I knew. She dreamed of being a mother since she had been fifteen. She would come pick up Emily on Thursday nights and keep her until Saturday. This was a help since I worked a twelve-hour shift on Friday. I would go over to her house on Friday evenings.

One Friday night when Emily turned five, my worst nightmare happened.

I was at home with Emily, and Brad and Alexandrea had somewhere to go. Emily was sitting in her wheelchair at the kitchen table with her chicken nuggets when I heard a phone call come in. I answered it, and it was my sister.

"If you won't do something about it, I will," was all I heard.

Chapter 4

(From this point on is Alexandrea's point of view.)

I couldn't wait to tell my mom; it was really happening. She was going to be a grandmother. I was really going to be a Momma and Brad a Daddy.

As we turned down my mother's street, I got the weirdest feeling I had ever felt. Brad pulled the car to a stop and killed the engine.

"What's wrong?" He caressed my face.

"I don't know. It's just my silly feelings at it again." But this time, they weren't off, at all. I had no idea what was coming and how my life was about to change forever. We walked in through the unlocked front door.

"Mom?" I called out. "Emily? Where are you, guys?"

I received taps from Emily, and I followed them. They were more dramatic than usual. She can't talk, so she uses taps to sometimes answer. What I saw in the kitchen gut-punched me, and I passed out. My husband picked me up off the ground and laid me on the sofa. He then went to Emily and took her in his arms. He sat on the couch with me until I came around, and we got out of the house. My mother was deceased on the kitchen floor, and Emily, other than whoever broke in, was the only one who knew anything. Emily had no way of telling us, other than using her taps to answer yes and no. We had to ask her the hard questions. Did she know the person? One tap meant no. The police wanted a description. How was I supposed to get that? I had come to share the best news of our life, and I had walked in on a daughter's worst nightmare.

It took hours of broken-up questioning, and then there was the funeral. Emily just sat in her wheelchair next our mother's coffin and stared. How could this be happening? I just wanted to get somewhere and cry my heart out, but there wasn't time. We had to find them before they got to Emily and us.

There was a note found in our mailbox, and it was dusted for fingerprints. Seeing a random piece of paper in our box, we didn't touch it due to surrounding circumstances. I called the detective on the case, and he came right over. I didn't know what to expect at this point, I guess anything or nothing, I don't know. Emily couldn't give me much with her taps. But what we did get was that she had seen the person—they had gray hair and blue eyes. That could be anyone from here to nowhere. This would probably become a cold case, but then Emily gave me something unexpected.

She went to the phone one day and tapped on it, unwavering. I asked her if she wanted to call someone, and she tapped once, hard, on the end table where the phone sat. I sat down and waited patiently.

She continued tapping on the telephone. My husband entered the room, and I quietly explained what was happening. He sat down and asked her a question that changed everything.

"Emily, was there someone on the phone before Mommy was killed?"

Two taps.

"Do you know who?" I prayed she could communicate it to us by God's amazing grace.

One tap. Emily did not know who had called. The detective was all over it when I called.

"We can pull phone records. We can find that out, Alex. We will."

It was my aunt Sharon.

Detective Gabriel Isaiah was one of the best on this side of Dallas. He would solve my mother's murder. I went through my brain and racked it for anyone who would want to hurt her. There were no boyfriends in the picture; my biological dad had been out of it years earlier. There were no friends, so-called, who had anything against her or she owed. Who would want to hurt mine and Emily's mother?

I went over this with Detective Isaiah a dozen times, if not more. We came up with nothing—disheartening.

One day, while working in my garden at seven months pregnant, it occurred to me there may have been someone we overlooked, someone we should look at. I called Detective Isaiah, and he was there on the double.

I kissed Emily as I put her down for her afternoon nap and closed her door. I had a baby monitor on in the living room, so I could see and hear her.

Detective Isaiah, my husband, and I sat at our small kitchen table, and there we tried to actually begin to crack this case. How could she? Did she? Why would she?

He had paid our aunt a visit. Sharon was not overly helpful. She did have an alibi. However, she did have a motive. She was jealous of her sister.

"I didn't like her adopting that kid, and still don't. I didn't think it was right for her. But I don't want her dead."

Like the detective said, "Jealousy is an ugly thing and could have been a motive for Sharon." Her alibi was rock and solid and getting stronger by the day. She had been at some function with hundreds of other people from town. Well, that was it. We had no leads, and my baby was due in less than three months. Emily still gave me signs; there was something she needed me to know, but neither she nor any of us knew what to do about it. Finally, a thought occurred to me one day while I was getting Emily ready for a doctor's appointment. We were three weeks out from the investigation on my aunt. I asked Emily if she knew who had been on the phone. She shook her head no. I tried once more. She did know who had killed our mother. It occurred to me for some reason to ask her if she knew where the person lived. Although I doubted it very strong since Emily was a child, she nodded. After the appointment, I asked her if she could show me. She could point at things. If it was someone we knew, I would know where they lived. I first turned down Poplar Av; she shook her head furiously. I turned around in farmer Ben Johnston's drive and waved to him and his wife, Milly. Then I headed over to North Main. That wasn't it either.

I paused in front of the coffee shop and wracked my brain. I didn't know where to go next. "Can you point me in the right direction, God?" I prayed.

Suddenly, she pointed right, so I headed north.

Chapter 5

Detective Gabriel Isaiah pulled his patrol car into his driveway, parked, and turned off the radio. As he turned off the key, he tried doing what he always did. He tried leaving work at work. Gabriel could normally do this, but not this one, not tonight. He saw that little girl in his mind and felt the urgency in his heart, as he got out and closed the door behind him, hitting the lock button. He prayed harder as he crossed his front lawn to his waiting wife at his front door. Her brunette hair rested on her shoulders.

"God, my family needs me present. Please help that family and help us crack that case. Thank You for getting me home safe. In Jesus's name I pray, amen." He prayed the last part silently as he slipped into the arms of his wife, Lucy. He ran his hands through her still-wet hair and kissed her cheek. She was wonderful. She took care of their six children, held down a job, and loved him—how had he gotten so wonderfully blessed by God.

He kissed his wife, and they headed inside. It was 10:00 p.m., so the younger kids were in bed. He took off his duty belt and rubbed his back. He showered and then slipped into his kids' rooms to pray over them and kiss their heads. KallieAnn, aged two, slept soundly with Miss Piggy at her side. He was glad he bought that. Mark Ryan, aged nine, was fast asleep in his Batman bed. He shared a room with Camdon Luke, aged twelve, who sat on the edge of his bed waiting on his dad. He hugged him, and Cam smiled.

"I made the basketball team."

He messed up his son's dark hair and smiled. "I'm proud of you son," he whispered so as not to wake his younger son. "I love you."

He met his fourteen-year-old daughter, Hannah Faith, in the hallway. Her dark hair laid in waves on her shoulders and down her back. Her blue eyes smiled at him. She shared a room with her younger sister. She made a wonderful older sister. He hugged her tight.

"I'm proud of you, Hannah. I love you, girl."

"I love you too, Dad. I made the cheerleading squad."

"I'm so proud of you. Good night, sweetheart. Sweet dreams."

"You too, Dad. I'm glad you are home."

"Me too, Hannah. It's been a long day that's made me miss you, kids, and Mom."

"We missed you too." She smiled as she slipped into her and Kallie's bedroom.

Aaron Shayne, aged 17, and Matthew James, aged 21, sat in the living room with their mother. He smiled at the picture they made, staring at the TV screen. He slipped up behind his wife and began rubbing her tense shoulders. He whispered that he loved her in her ear, and she switched off the TV.

"Enough bad news for one night."

"How was your day, Dad?" Aaron asked. He was interested in following in his dad's footsteps.

"Interesting to say the least. I'll have to say, it's a tough case to figure out when your star witness can only speak through taps and movement of head."

"Taps?" Lucy asked.

"It's a long story. Just pray for the family. That's all I can really say."

"That's the most important thing." Lucy sighed, taking his hand.

* * * * *

I closed my eyes, Emily was still sleeping, and Brad had left for work. I had the big nursing state test coming up tomorrow. Would

I pass it? I was glad to be done with school, and Emily was at a calm stretch with her seizures. For the most part, she could eat what she liked.

I prayed as I did every morning that today would be the day. It made me uneasy not knowing if our mother's killer wanted us too.

As I fed Emily her oatmeal, the doorbell rang. I waddled over to the door and saw Detective Isaiah standing on my porch. "Detective, come in." I opened the door wide. "Are there any leads?" I proceeded to finish feeding Emily.

"Not yet." He tickled Emily on the shoulder, and she grinned. Grinning was something she didn't do much these days. Mom was her world.

"She is smiling for you." That made me smile despite the burning questions that were never far from my tongue.

"Well let's see if this Officer Bear makes her smile." He placed the bear in Emily's lap. At first, she just sat motionless. I waited for her to knock Officer Bear on the floor, like she usually did with some types of toys. Slowly, she touched its soft fur and then eased it to her face. She made a move with her lips like she wanted to say something.

"You are so welcome, sweetheart," the kind officer spoke as if he were understanding Emily's unspoken words. "I just wanted to come by to give this to Emily from the department and also to tell you that your aunt has been cleared."

"Really?" Now, it was my turn to sit motionless. "Now, where do we go from here?"

"Well," he smiled down at Emily, "I was hoping you and Emily could show me where that house was, the one she pointed to the other day."

I knew the one. I'd called Detective Isaiah as soon as Em had pointed out the house the other morning. "Sure," I stood, "Let me get her dressed and in the van."

Once on the road, I wracked my brain. This couldn't be happening, could it? Were me and Emily really showing a detective to my first cousin's house? Well, really, it was my uncle's house, but he let his son Jonas live there for free. Jonas Marcom wasn't someone I wanted to be around or expose Emily to. But he should be at work at this hour, if he still worked. I gripped the wheel and placed a call through the car to my husband. He was a little nerve-wracked when I told him what was going on.

Detective Isaiah had said the crime lab had DNA and they had the prints from the house. They just needed a match for the prints on the door handle. My mom had clearly fault because the intruder's skin was found under her fingernails along with his or her hair—scary. It was a miracle we still had Emily.

I turned into the neighborhood and pulled off in an empty house's pathed driveway. I wished we could do that to ours. Detective Isaiah walked up to Emily's window, and I rolled it down. Recording, he asked her to show him the house where the person lives, who killed her mommy.

I held my breath, but Emily followed through.

Chapter 6

Just as he'd thought, Detective Isaiah crossed his arms and groaned. He stared at his supervisor, Darren.

"I still think he is connected to so many more."

"Like your wife's cousin?"

"Yeah, I do, but yeah. That has been twenty-five years ago, and it's a cold case now. Could we see if the prints match? What would it hurt?"

"What, and check all the others too? I guess," his supervisor muttered. "Don't be disappointed if you don't crack it. It happens."

Was that what he thought? Well of course he would be disappointed. He was planning to retire in six weeks, and this had been his mission, one of them anyway. He wanted to figure out who killed Shawndra twenty-five years earlier. But at the moment, he had to find the guy.

"Yea, I do think we should have them all checked for a match."

"Fine," the man glared at him, "but don't be disappointed."

The guy, Jonas Marcum, should be getting home about now, and Gabriel was waiting, waiting and praying. He had to catch him to bring him in for questioning and a DNA sample. He wanted to be a light to the man, and maybe he was innocent of everything. Finally, twenty minutes later, a silver sedan drove into the driveway of the rundown house. He matched the plate to what they had on file, and the man at wheel fit the man's description to the tee.

"Jonas Marcum?" Gabriel said slowly, stepping from his car, while the man did the same—tall, stocky, dark-brown hair, and could have a knife or something.

"Yes, what do you want from me?"

"You are not under arrest, but please place your hands on the vehicle so I can make sure you don't have anything on you for my safety and yours."

The man did as he was asked, and the compliance worked in both their favors.

"I'm Detective Isaiah. I'm going to need you to come with me for some questioning."

"Questioning for what exactly? Man, look, I have plans tonight. So you are going to have to wait."

"That won't be happening," Detective Isaiah said in a kind patient tone. "I can't let you go. I have orders to bring you in."

For all they knew, he could be a flight risk, at least, a runaway risk. Gabriel didn't lean toward flight risk as much, but he wasn't going to let this man slide between his grasps.

"Fine." The man climbed into the back of Detective Isaiah's police car and didn't look happy about it, at all.

Once in the interrogation room, Detective Isaiah gave the man a Coca-Cola and a pack of crackers. "Thought you might be hungry. You just got off work, right?"

"Yea." The man ate the crackers and chugged the drink.

Detective Isaiah had let his wife, Lucy, know he would be a while and not to wait up or hold dinner. He sat in a calm posture and kept a neutral face. "I can tell that you are nervous," he said to the man across from him.

"Why do you say it? Why am I nervous? I have nothing to be nervous about." His hazel-green, at the moment very dark eyes darted the span of the room.

"Do you not? Where were you on the night of February 21? Say between 5:00 and 6:00 p.m.?"

"I don't remember." The guy crossed his arms and shook his head vigorously. This wasn't going well. "Really, seriously? Do you think I remember that?"

"Yes, I do." Detective Gabriel did not lose his cool or his calm posture. He just went another step further. "Do you know a woman by the name of Versie Gail Pennacheck?"

"Of course, I do. She's my aunt. She has a daughter and some kid she adopted. Kid has problems."

Gabriel had to bite his tongue on that one. Emily was the sweetest child and deserved the same respect as everyone else did. He knew his wife, Lucy, would just love her. Detective Isaiah tried once more. "Where were you between five and six on this evening? It's important, and while you think on that, be prepared to give us a DNA sample."

"Why?" The man's eyes went dark. He got that wait-a-minute look.

"You don't think I killed her? Come on, man."

"I don't know what to think unless you give me something to go on. You are not answering my question. Where were you?"

"I was busy."

"Doing what?"

"That's for me to know and you to find out?"

What did that mean?

"Had you rather just give us the sample? Do you want a lawyer, as I have already asked? Your call."

"Yea, I'll give you the sample. But you can't hold me right? I'm not under arrest?"

"Why won't you tell me where you were busy at? Come on, Marcum, help me here."

"I was taking care of some business."

"Help yourself out. What kind of business?"

Now they might be getting somewhere.

"I was…running an errand for…a friend. Yeah."

"Where?"

* * * * *

After ten hours, they still didn't have enough to hold him. Detective Gabriel went home and crawled in bed next to his wife. "God, we need a miracle and those DNA sample results back."

Finally, the lab had the results. He was a match; he was really a match. He wondered how to tell Alex. Surprise hit him that Marcum had been willing to give the sample; he had to know it would not come back clean.

Chapter 7

I sat at our small dining room table, wracking my brain. It had been just two days ago that Detective Isaiah had come and told me the news. But now, the person that the news was about was missing. So far, they had connected him to thirty crimes in the last twenty-eight years. So where was he, and why hadn't they held him were the exact questions I asked the kind and patient detective.

"Well," he gave me an understanding look, "where he is, is what I want to know also. Why we didn't hold him? We did not have enough to hold him at the time of his interrogation. I'm sorry. I can tell this is stressing you out and rightly so. We have amped up patrol around your home. I'm praying without ceasing."

"Thanks. Me too. God is our only hope at this point."

There was no need to say what I was thinking out loud because I could tell the detective was thinking the same thing.

* * * * *

That night at home, Gabriel couldn't focus. He couldn't stop thinking about Alex, Emily, Brad, and their entire family really. The fact he had really been a match didn't really surprise Gabriel. But how the guy had gotten by with it all these years did go beyond him. His superior had given him an apology and told him he was surprised he was a match to all the murders. They planned to compare all cases more closely later, in an attempt to see what had been missed. Thank

God for DNA and giving man the knowledge to learn how to do what they did.

He kissed his wife after supper and told her how good it was as they shared a cup of coffee. He also whispered to her how pretty she looked. Then, he asked each of his kids about their day. Hanah had a test that Friday that she was real concerned about. He told her to meet him at the kitchen table at seven with popcorn, and they would study together. His son Matthew had a flat on his pickup. So before he headed for his evening job, they headed out to fix a flat. After the new tire was securely in place, they sat on the porch swing for only a moment.

"Dad?" Matthew looked at him with serious eyes.

"Yes?" He was listening fully to his son.

"What am I going to do with myself?"

"What do you mean?" his dad asked with a chuckle.

"What am I supposed to do with myself? I don't have a degree and don't really honestly have a clue where to go from here. I'm not worth much."

"Now, hold on there." His dad slipped an arm around his shoulders to give his son a hug. "You are worth everything to me. I wouldn't take a million dollars for you, not a million or any amount."

His son hung his head for a moment and then raised it again to look at his dad. "I love you, Dad."

"I love you too, Matt. Thanks for being you, and doing your best is all I can ask of you. Your mother and I are proud of the man you have and are becoming."

Later that night, after Hannah understood her history a little better, he had played a round of baseball with Mark Ryan and played baby dolls with Kallie Ann. He smiled. Aaron waited at the top of the stairs for him. "Dad?"

"Son?"

"I know that's what I want. I want to be in law enforcement."

"That's good. Finish high school, and then we will go from there. You will make a good one. But you aren't just doing it because I am, are you?"

"No, yes, no. I mean, you are my hero, and I want to be like you. But that's the direction I am hearing from God to go."

"Then run. Prayers always for you, son, prayers for safety and guidance because you are going to need lots of it. Learn the law, and care about people. Always, and I mean always, listen to *God's* voice. You cannot and will not go wrong that way."

"Thanks, Dad. I love you."

"And I love you." He realized he hadn't seen much of Camdon that evening. So he climbed the stairs after Aaron and opened Camdon's door.

"Cam?" he whispered.

His twelve-year-old son raised his head up and whispered back, "Yea?"

"You okay, son? Haven't seen much of you this evening."

"Long day, Dad. Percilla won't talk to me."

Wasn't this liking-each-other thing getting younger by the year? "Son," he sat on the edge of Cam's bed, "you are young, and she is young. What happened?" Then he had a sickening feeling this had nothing to do with a crush. Why? He didn't know.

"No, Dad, it isn't like that. She's being bullied and is shutting down to everyone. They have kicked the bullies out of school, well, suspended them a few times. But a lot of it is done where no one sees. They pull her hair and tell her she's ugly, and I heard one of them say they would have a group of girls catch her in the bathroom and do something. Dad, I don't know what to do."

"You just did the right thing by telling me. I will contact the school resource officer tonight, in fact right now. Who are the bullies?" After he had contacted the SRO, Jackie, he found Lucy folding laundry in the living room.

"Come on," he gently took hold of her arm, "that can wait until tomorrow."

She looked up at him. "Okay?" She put down the wash rag she was holding. "Spill it? What is on your mind? You have been a million miles away while still being here."

"Just ten or so. Let's go on the porch." He told her a little of what he could. "The guy is on the loose now, and I am highly concerned for them, Lucy. I know God is in control and can do more than I can. It just seems like there should have been something to hold him on. But this guy is good, and that scares me a little."

"Does he know where we live? Like—"

He put his finger to her lips and then kissed her. "I hope not."

As they got ready to climb into bed, a feeling, an urgency, pushed him to turn on his police radio. He didn't usually do that at night, but tonight, he did. In five minutes, it came to life.

"Dispatch all available units." Mary Ann was the dispatcher. "Respond signal 42 to 49 Lanover Drive."

He immediately recognized the address.

"1049 in progress. Caller says the intruder is attempting to gain access now."

He wasn't on duty, but he was now.

"Lucy, I gotta go. That's Alex, Brad, and Emily, the little girl who taps."

"Why?"

"I'll explain later. Just pray. Now, pray, and don't stop. I love you."

"Be careful. I, we, love you too."

She kissed him, and he promptly returned her kiss. He squeezed her in a hug, threw on his gear including his vest, and ran for the door. Once in his police cruiser, he turned the key. Nothing happened. "Come on, PLEASE, DEAR GOD! I need to go." It was then he remembered the jumper cables in the back. He rushed inside, woke up Matt, and got his keys.

Matt came to help, and in minutes, they had it running. "I love you, Dad. Be careful."

"I will, son. I love you too." He was on the road, lights and siren, and on the phone with his boss.

"Isaiah?" he answered with his thick Salt Lake accent. "Up kind of late, aren't you?"

"Uh yea, headed for Lanover."

"Why? We can handle it—"

"No, this is personal."

* * * * *

I had been lying in bed next to Emily. She had a bed in mine and Brad's bedroom. It was easier that way. Emily was restless, and I was with her. There wasn't much sleeping at eight months pregnant.

I heard a sound and held my breath. It could have been the cat, but then again, no, that was definitely not the cat.

"Brad," I whispered, "Brad! Wake up. Someone is here."

In seconds, he was on his feet. We had almost expected this. Not that we didn't believe God would protect us, but He gives us the knowledge to pay attention to our surroundings. The next thing I knew, I was hearing the sound I had prayed I'd never hear—glass shuddering along with the sound of our alarm system bellering through the broken silence of the night.

Chapter 8

As soon as Detective Isaiah pulled on the scene, he noticed two things right away: the front door was smashed in, and a car was speeding in the opposite direction that he came. He threw the car in reverse and sped after the creep. His heart raced as he called in pursuit. The car took a hard right-hand turn.

"Dear God!" Gabriel yelled.

It was only by the amazing grace of the Almighty God that the man kept the sedan on the highway. The sedan—he related the silver sedan's plate and description into his radio as they sped down a back road that Gabriel wasn't familiar with. It split off into two different directions, and due to his not knowing the road, he was five seconds too late. "Dear God, protect that innocent child. Please, God! And lead us to her."

* * * * *

I sat on the couch sick and panicked. *Where was Emily?* Before either of us had the chance to do anything, he or she had grabbed her, our baby. *What were we going to do?*

The person had broken in through our front door, and face covered in a mask and dressed in black, they busted into our bedroom and grabbed Emily. My husband ran after the person, but being knocked off his feet by the intruder made him a couple of steps slower. The only other thing missing, besides my sister, was her medicine.

Detective Isaiah came back with a defeated look on his face. He had tried to save Emily, and I knew that because I had seen him pull in. Then, I'd watched him go after the guy.

"Alex," he sat down next to me, "give me a good description of Emily and a recent photo. Also, what was she waring and any distinguishing features? We have a bolo and ATL out to all agencies. We will also release an Amber Alert to the public."

I tried to remember everything he just said.

"A pink mermaid nightgown, her favorite. She had socks on, white, with pink flowers on them." I watched my husband breathe in sharply. He had given a good description.

"Her arm. Her right arm is stiff, and she really can't move it. If her medicine isn't given properly," I croaked out.

"And on time," my husband shrieked.

"Yea," I gasped, "it will be very bad."

"We'll find her, Alex, Brad."

I stared into kind eyes of someone who wasn't just a detective; he was a dad. I knew because he had told us about his wife and six kids at home. They were praying for us, and we for them. I closed my eyes and then felt something. No, not now! I informed my husband, and with the assurance of the hardworking law enforcement that they would find Emily, we headed for the hospital. Eighteen hours later, our son, Jacob Brad, was born. But we still had no trace of Emily.

* * * * *

Exhausted, but sure, Detective Isaiah headed for the hospital. He had realized a very important key might be missing. He also wanted to inform Alex of the discovery they had made with the help of God. They had discovered there had actually been two intruders at her home last night, not only one.

The feeling in the pit of his stomach nearly brought him to his knees. *What if his feeling was right? Did they still have the video from the day Emily was abandoned at dispatch?* He needed some answers from Alex and Brad. He was almost there, but he needed to make a call to the office and see if that video was in evidence. *Could whoever was biologically connected to Emily be responsible, even partly?*

He hung up. He put the car in park, climbed out, and glanced around. It was a habit. *But what if at this very moment whoever was responsible was watching with the satisfaction they had uprooted someone's life?*

This should be a happy time for Brad and Alex. Upon entering the room, he found Alex, Brad, and some other family members gathered around the most precious little baby.

"A boy I see." The detective smiled. This took him back to the births of his own kids.

"Hi, Detective Isaiah." Alex smiled and made the introductions.

He shook hands with some other family members and handed the couple a gift from he, Lucy, and the kids. Then, he got down to business. "I am sorry to have to do this, but I need to ask you and Brad some questions. The family is welcome to stay if you want them too."

They gave the signal to their family to stay and nodded to Gabriel.

"Okay then. Were you all able to learn the identification of who abandoned Emily?"

"You don't think?" Alex's mouth fell open.

"I'm not sure if they are connected in some way, but I want to check if possible."

* * * * *

I held my son and prayed, not just regular prayers; I was praying with every fiber in me that my Emily was safe. My heart hurt. I could feel my mother's arms, which would have been around me had she been here. I could hear Emily's taps, trying to show us. Could that guy, our cousin, be involved? We had no idea who her biological parents were or who had dropped her there. I'm just glad they did, and I wanted her back in my arms today. I felt the urge to question why, but God is not the author of confusion. The devil is.

Three days later, we were home with our son. But still, they hadn't found our Emily. Detective Isaiah had told me with a brokenness that was palpable and that in most cases, if not found in the first twenty-four hours, there isn't usually a good outcome. He also said something that would stick with me forever: "Alex, God only knows what lies ahead. It doesn't matter what statistics say, but we will keep praying until Emily is found, and after that."

Chapter 9

Gabriel Isaiah was tired, but he wasn't giving up. Five weeks until retirement, and right about now, it loomed like a dark cloud over him. He had to solve this case, now, not only for Shondra but for a little girl with black pigtails named Emily.

Alex had said something was missing that really sparked his interest into finding Emily's biological parents. He hadn't stopped watching that house since Thursday evening. At least, he'd had eyes on it. When Jonas Marcum came home, they'd be waiting. His cell phone rang at that point, and it was his boss.

"Hello," he answered with the hope of answers looming.

"Isaiah, your gut was on point. Marcum is Emily's biological dad."

"Now," Gabriel rubbed his temples, "where's the mother? I've got a gut feeling she's in danger."

* * * * *

Alex rocked her son and prayed. She prayed with a gut-wrenching feeling that Emily was no longer with them. Right at this very second, there were God only knew how many emergency personnel and volunteers from town searching and combing a stretch of woods. It was a tip that'd come in.

"It could be nothing," Detective Isaiah had told her, "but it could be something. We follow up on them all."

Her husband had gone to help look, leaving her home alone with the baby. She thought of calling her friend, Morgen, to come over, but no, they'd be fine, no need to involve Morgen when she'd just lost her dad three weeks ago. She had three young sons of her own at home to care for. So Alex just rocked and prayed. Around an hour after her husband had left to help look, the electric went out, and that's strange.

* * * * *

Gabriel wiped the sweat from off his brow as Brad walked up to him with a defeated look on his face. There was something else there too—fear maybe?"

"I'm so sorry this was another dead end, Brad."

They'd followed three more leads before this and sadly came up with nothing. Jonas Marcum still hadn't showed up at his house or work either for that matter.

"Brad, what's wrong?" Gabriel's stomach went to his knees, and his heart started praying for mercy.

"Alex and the baby. The electric went out, and someone is banging on the front door." The front door they'd only just repaired.

"Get in, you can ride with me. Stay in the car when we get there though." Gabriel hit the gas, the lights, and the siren. Half a dozen other police vehicles followed behind him. His chief was among them.

As soon as they pulled on the scene, Gabriel yelled for Brad to get down and called into the radio to inform dispatch of shots fired.

* * * * *

Alex and the baby hid in the bathroom. It seemed like the best place, since there were no windows. Right now, upon hearing what she just had, that really was rather appealing.

"Dear God," she cried as the first shot rang out. Her baby was sleeping in her arms, and she could feel his soft skin. She could feel and hear the racing of her own heartbeat. She prayed for everyone's safety. It was then the gut-wrenching realization hit her square in the gut that she had no clue where her husband was. The thought was fitting; they had no clues on Emily either. She chided herself, at least none that had panned out anyway.

"Dear God, I can't lose him too. Please help us."

She kept praying as she listened to five or more shots ring out. In a few minutes, she heard her front door open, with a key. She realized she was shaking uncontrollably. In moments, she was in Brad's arms, and Detective Isaiah was holding out his arms to cradle her son.

* * * * *

Gabriel groaned as he climbed in his car and headed for the hospital. The man had managed to slip from their almost grip. He had been hiding around the side of the house; when they pulled in, he came around firing five shots. His officer brother, Matt, had fired after the man, but he disappeared before anyone could see where he went.

For the next hour, they searched Alex and Brad's property, which turned up nothing. Other officers combed the area's surrounding. For the time, Alex, Brad, and the baby were moved to a safe spot. There had been no vehicle present, at least not that Alex or they heard or saw.

He prayed his chief would live. The guy could add more charges as of now to his long list, and if the chief died, well that told the story.

Lucy joined him at the hospital.

"Hi." She sat down to his right.

He breathed in her sweet scent. He was glad she was off today; she would probably have worked the run. She held out a cup of coffee to him, and he took it. He drank half of it down and sat it on the table to his left.

"The kids?" He kissed her and took her hand.

"Fine. They are with my sis having dinner. I wanted to be here, with you. Is he going to live, Gabriel?"

"I certainly pray so."

"Where are Alex, Brad, and their little baby?"
"At a secret location, which can't be disclosed."

* * * * *

Alex watched Brad walk the floor with the baby in his arms. It had nothing to do with their son not sleeping. "Honey, walking a whole in the floor won't help save us. Come sit, and let's pray."

He paused only a moment. "I know that will help, Alex, and I trust God. I'm just hurting right now, as are you, and it's hard to pray."

"All I can say is help me, help us, please save Emily, dear sweet Jesus! I don't feel safe here, Brad."

"It's better than home."

Alex knew that he was right; she just couldn't shake the feeling that something was not right. "Dear God, where is Emily?"

* * * * *

Gabriel slid from his and his wife's bed the next morning. He dawned his uniform and badge and his vest—always the vest. It could be the deciding factor if he went home or not that day. He slipped downstairs and flipped the switch to make the coffee.

He yawned, picked up the paper, unfolded it, and then put it back. He didn't need to read the front page to know the story. Emily's picture graced the page. He dropped to the nearest chair and started his prayer. For the next thirty minutes, he prayed. The coffee could wait.

After he finished breakfast and his coffee, he slid quietly out the front door. It being Saturday, Lucy and the kids were still sleeping. His task today was to shield Brad, Alex, and the baby while they were moved to a new location. They had been found. Gabriel and the others were sure of it. And judging by the note on his patrol car, he might need to take Lucy and their six kids with them to safety.

* * * * *

Alex felt strange making scrambled eggs and knowing security was just outside. This had to be some kind of twisted nightmare, isn't it? She wasn't making breakfast for she and Brad in a safe house and Emily wasn't missing, right?

She shoved the question aside with a huff. It was real, and she had to deal with it. Her mother was dead, and she had to face that too. The fact that whoever had taken her sister was probably who murdered her mother was a fact she also couldn't ignore either. So yeah, she had to pray, right now. If it wasn't for the mighty hand of God holding her up, she was sure she would have crumbled by just about now. Not to mention they had to move again, and ditch their phones, because they might be tracking them. What?

* * * * *

"You are next. Your family—"

His family what? He wasn't taking any chances; he had to get them and move, now. Gabriel contacted his boss and informed him that his family would be coming to the safe house too.

"You know we can't do that, Gabriel."

"We can when we are in danger too." He read the man the note. He huffed and gave Gabriel the clearance he needed.

"But when you are there, stay put, all of you."

* * * * *

Lucy was flabbergasted. What was going on? Why was Gabe waking her at five-thirty in the morning and telling her to pack things and "let's go"? She obeyed, and together, they woke up their children. Lucy threw some things in a bag for she and the younger two and helped the others. She threw Gabriel's things in too and prayed for guidance. She wanted to be honest with her kids but didn't want them to be afraid.

"Help me, God, to know how to handle this. Keep me calm so my children will stay calm. Help Gabriel and the others know what to do. Help Alex and her family."

They were out of time. The officers who were going to be escorting them had arrived.

Let the nightmare begin, Lucy thought and then started to pray once more.

* * * * *

"Do you think they know where we are now?" Alex pushed the words out from the back seat of an unmarked car.

"We hope not," came the short, clipped words of the detective in the driver's seat.

For only a moment, she thought she saw fear in his eyes. He hid it well, though. Brad squeezed her hand. He sat on the other side of their son, who slept soundly in his car seat, oblivious to what was taking place. She bent over and nuzzled her nose to his. "Dear God, please keep us safe." She trusted God; she really did. *He* was their only hope of getting out from this alive.

Brad slid his fingers around hers, lifted them to his lips, and kissed them softly. "It's going to be okay, Al. It has to be."

* * * * *

Gabriel and three of their kids were put into one unmarked tinted-window SUV and Lucy and the other three children into another unmarked tinted-window SUV. Gabriel's gut clenched. He hated being separate. They would be at the safe house in less than thirty minutes. He watched behind them, just watched the car his wife and three of their kids rode in, praying God would see them safely there and then that God would keep anyone from finding them at least who shouldn't.

Chapter 10

Once inside the safe house, Gabriel and Lucy made sure every window was covered. Lucy would have preferred the windows be covered in bulletproof steel or something, but since they didn't have that, they would pray for a shield from God. That was her prayer in all this, for everyone. They would just have to pray no one found them and stay away from the windows. God's shield was stronger than any other.

Gabriel paced and prayed. The children understandably started asking questions.

"Dear God, help me stay strong," Lucy prayed.

Together, she and Gabriel tried to answer every one of their questions. Lucy wished for a strong cup of coffee, but she didn't have any.

Just as they got Kallie Ann to sit calmly in her daddy's lap, the front door opened, with a key. Two deputies walked in with Alex, Brad, and the baby boy.

"Are we having a sleepover?" Kallie beamed.

"Kind of." Hannah attempted a smile. "Better than the alternative." Her daughter had said the last so quiet that no one else probably heard her.

Lucy slid an arm around her daughter's shoulders. "Thank you for helping your little sister. I love you."

"I'm trying to help me from panicking too."

"We all are, honey. Pray, talk to Jesus, and don't stop, sweetheart."

* * * * *

I was glad to see another female. But I was confused why they were there. Once settled, I would ask Gabriel's wife. Maybe they'd become permanent friends. "If we made it through all this," I chided myself. I had to trust God. *He* always takes care of us.

I made a bottle for the baby and put it to his lips. He began sucking, at least that was normal. I closed my eyes and then realized just how tired and exhausted I was.

"Would you like some help?" a gentle voice broke through my thoughts.

I opened them to see Gabriel's sweet wife standing in front of me. I gave her a smile and shifted the baby higher in my arms. He had apparently slid down, and I hadn't known it. Had I fallen asleep?

"Hi." I yawned. "Did I fall asleep?"

"Just slightly. Would you like me to hold him for you so that you can get rest? I know your exhausted."

I paused and trusted her with my son. She had six of her own, so I said, "Would you? Thank you. I am exhausted."

"What's his name? He is so precious." She held out her arms, and I gave her my son, his blanket, and bottle.

"Jacob, and thank you."

Brad walked over and covered me with a blanket and then slid a pillow beneath my head.

"Thanks," I managed to say before drifting off for a restless sleep of a couple of hours.

* * * * *

Lucy held the baby. She could never get enough of little ones. Kallie Ann crawled up beside her, and Gabriel was on her heels.

"Isn't he so sweet?" Gabriel whispered in her ear.

"He is." Lucy nuzzled her face to this soft baby.

"Can we keep him, Mommy?" Kallie asked.

Gabriel and Lucy giggled.

"Not hardly," Lucy said. "His Daddy and Momma love him very much."

The older kids took their turns holding the baby. Finally, it was lunchtime. Lucy, knowing her family was hungry, went to search the kitchen. Surprised to find it fully stocked, she went to work.

* * * * *

I woke to a sweet smell filling my nose. *What was that? Wait, fried chicken.* I stood, found a bathroom, and then found my husband and son in the kitchen with everyone else.

"Lucy made lunch." Brad stood and kissed me.

"I see that, and it smells wonderful."

What appeared to be their next to oldest held Jacob. I smiled at him and began making my plate.

"You are a good babysitter."

"I've had lots of practice." He laughed.

The fact that any of us could laugh was a miracle at this point. Soon, my plate was filled with fried chicken, mashed potatoes, green beans, and a roll. "Where did you all get this?"

"The kitchen was actually stocked," Lucy smiled, "thankfully."

"Momma is a good cook," their oldest son said. "Hi, I'm Matthew."

"Glad to meet all of you, sad that it's under these circumstances however."

Lucy and Gabriel introduced their children. The two officers even talked about their families. Things seemed to be going well, too well, until that night.

As we all found places to sleep that night, Brad and I on a pallet with the baby, I had an eerie feeling. *We were safe, right? No one knew where we were, right?* I started praying and quoting familiar Bible scripture. It helped, and soon, I was asleep.

* * * * *

Gabriel and Lucy slept in the only bedroom, with all their children on pallets on the floor. They figured Kallie would end up in bed with them, but for now, she was sleeping with her sis. Lucy laid her head on Gabriel's arm.

"Dear God, let us get out of this alive please, dear LORD," she prayed silently.

"Amen," Gabriel whispered from beside her.

How had he done that, known she was praying? "What?"

"I was saying amen to whatever prayer you were praying."

She loved this man. She reached up and tilted his head so she could kiss him. "I love you, Gabriel."

"I love you, Lucy."

It was about that time the night-light plugged in the wall went out, and so did the air conditioner.

"I don't like this," Gabriel whispered.

Lucy didn't either. A noise shot Gabriel to a sitting position. Someone was rattling the doorknob loud enough to hear it through the closed bedroom door, and they wanted in.

Chapter 11

"Brad," I whispered.

"I hear it." He froze.

Voices—I heard voices. Detective Isaiah came out of the bedroom and shut the door. He went to the front window, standing to the side, and looked out. I wondered what he saw. Before I could ask, a crashing noise came from the bedroom and a scream.

Detective Isaiah, Brad, and the two officers ran with someone slamming open the bedroom door.

"Dear God," Detective Isaiah cried. He disappeared into the room and with a terrified but strong tone demanded, "Let her go!"

* * * * *

Gabriel had to do something but knew in his heart that he was fighting a losing battle.

"Dear God, do something. Please, God. You've brought us this far. I can't lose her now or Hannah." He grabbed for his weapon but realized it was on the nightstand; he hoped it was anyway. He hoped the person hadn't found it.

Lucy let out a screech, and he heard something connect with something else. Someone let out a low moan, and he heard the window close.

"Apparently," she said, breathing hard, "it wasn't closed good. He fell climbing in, and he fell going out."

He ran to his wife and daughter, and one of the officers flipped on the light switch. Of course, it was no use. There was no electricity.

"We have to get out of here," one of the officers said.

"I'm all for that." Gabriel agreed.

"How'd they find us?" Lucy asked, still shaking.

Gabriel's exact question.

"We are going to find out," the other officer replied, "Good footwork there, by the way."

"Thanks."

They loaded everyone up, and they were moved to another location. The officer in charge had gotten a burner phone; they had all had to ditch their cell phones. Lucy knew her family would be sick with worry, and she hated that. But right at the moment, they had to do what they had to do. It wasn't an issue where they were going, just if anyone found them.

Gabriel cringed at being separated again. But there just wasn't enough room in one vehicle. This time, Alex, the baby, Lucy, and three of their kids rode with two officers. Brad and their other three kids rode with Gabe and two other officers.

Gabe pressed his fingers to his eyes. How had they found them? They had, and now, they had to handle that. They were traveling under the cover of night, so hopefully, that would be of some help, but probably not with these guys or whoever they were. Somebody had a sore tail or ribs, maybe some bruises too. That could be to an advantage, if they could figure out where he was. Gabe had a pretty good idea who Lucy kicked from the window. She was probably sore too, and Hannah's wrist really needed to be looked at. The suspect had grabbed her pretty hard, prompting Lucy to act without any warning to the surprised intruder. He closed his eyes and prayed.

* * * * *

Truth was, I was tired, tired as in tired like a new mother and tired as in tired as in a sister who had no clue as to whether her little sister was even still alive. I was tired of running. I wanted to catch the killer and knock him down myself, like a foot to the jaw.

I was in a separate car from Brad, and I was glad Lucy was with me. Her younger kids rode in the back. I just prayed we got there safely. We noticed the officers watching the mirrors. Lucy kept her cool, but I could see the dark fear in her eyes. But I also saw the pure trust there, and I drew on it.

* * * * *

Gabriel had to convince them to let him help. He was protecting his family and Brad, Alex, and the baby, but it was hard for him to stay put. He wanted to look for Emily, and he wanted to find him, Marcum. He'd always looked for him, the person who caused all this. He let out a low groan, which must have been audible. Brad turned to look at him, and so did Matt.

"Dad?" Matt gave him a staring gaze.

"What are you thinking?" Brad asked.

"I don't know. Just that we have got to get this guy before he strikes again."

"How are we going to do that when we don't know where he is?" Mark asked from the front seat.

Gabriel ignored his shrill cold tone. He understood. "I feel the same way."

"We all do." Benny put in from the driver's seat. "I think we all are asking that question, even just to our self. I need to turn here. What is that truck doing?" Sure enough, a green truck blocked their way of turning. It wasn't stalled, but the driver was stalling them.

Lucy's gut clenched. This felt all too familiar. There was nothing wrong with that truck, but the driver was purposely blocking them. That meant they'd been found, again. But how? Lucy had a sickening feeling that she didn't want to acknowledge. But she did, and she was glad she had.

"Kids, get on the floor." She turned and unbuckled Kallie's seat and climbed in the back with her kids.

"Lucy, what are you doing?" the female officer driving the SUV asked.

"Alex, get the baby on the floor."

Alex obeyed, and about that time, it began. She could only pray her husband had the same memo in the vehicle in front of her.

Chapter 12

Gabe had a gnawing feeling to tell his kids to get on the floor. Despite the looks of the officers up front, he listened to God. "Kids, Brad, get down on the floor now! Dear God, let Lucy think and feel the same thing You are showing me. Please get us out of this alive." The prayer was for him and God alone, but out loud he said, "Pray, and pray hard."

It was about that time, a heart-throbbing voice came across the radio. "Get down. He has a gun."

Gabe watched Matt scramble over the seat to where his younger brothers were. He pushed them to the floor and laid on top of them. His heart swelled and sank all at once.

"Stolen, the plate is stolen."

The announcement came from Benny; he knew the information from dispatch over the radio. Gabe armed his weapon. The guy was out of the truck now and standing in the road. *Was he crazy? Never mind, bad question.*

The guy took off, and officers were on his tail. He prayed they'd catch the guy and let him have first dibs at questioning the creep. *Why was he doing this?*

Thirteen short but grueling minutes later, they arrived at the next safe point. It was a small place, but enough to regroup and figure out a permanent refuge. A couple of hours later, when they were finally at the new safe house, Lucy breathed a sigh of momentary relief. Then, with everyone exhausted, it was bedtime. No telling how long the quiet would last, so everyone relished it.

About five hours later, eleven in the morning, there was a knock at the door. Gabriel snuggled closer to Lucy, knowing the officers would handle it. They would know soon enough if there was trouble.

* * * * *

No question, there was trouble. I sat up, clutching the baby to my chest. Brad did the same and slid an arm around me. I shivered, no relation to the temperature in the safe house. *Did I really just have the thought Safe house? Ugh.*

* * * * *

Gabriel slid out of bed and went into the hallway. There were five rooms in this safe house. He, Lucy, and Kallie Ann shared one. Hannah shared one with her little brother Mark, who was scared stiff. In the next was Matt, Camron, and Aaron. Alex, Brad, and the baby shared the one at the end of the hall. Gabriel just stood there, listening.

"We've lost sight of them," Gabe heard Timmy, one of the officers, say.

What did he mean, lost sight of them? He didn't know but intended to find out. He stepped in the living room, as glass shuddering sent him running back in the direction he came. The bedroom doors flew open. Everyone was fine, seemingly.

"He must have come in the spare bedroom window." Lucy pointed. "Look!"

"Get back in the bedrooms, and lock up," Officer Kenton whispered.

"It's too late," a voice hissed. "Don't move, and do just as I say, and everyone will be just fine."

"Dear God," Detective Isaiah prayed, "he's got us now."

* * * * *

I saw two figures step out from the bedroom not in use. One, the taller of the two, wore a ski mask. The other one, more slender, dressed in all black, had something covering her face as well. She was shaking. I watched her, and she watched me. I watched Lucy's face, and it was pure fear and anger. She clutched Kallie Ann in her arms, and I could see the other kids wanted to get closer to their parents. But no one moved. For several seconds, we could hear the sound of the fridge running, everyone breathing, and the late morning sounds coming through the open window, the window where they probably planned to escape, with their victims.

****

"Dear God, help us!" Gabriel and the two other officers were praying and pulling on every bit of training. There were two suspects, and three of them, but the two came prepared.

"Put your guns down," the taller of them ordered.

"Not a chance," the officer nearest to Gabriel sternly replied and raised his weapon higher.

A bullet whizzed past Gabe's head, and he ducked. Lucy screamed.

"Shut up," the taller man ordered. "That was just a warning. Put the guns down. Now! Or I'll shoot again."

The three looked at one another. They laid their guns on the floor at their feet. Gabe noticed Matt slowly moving in front of his siblings. His heart swelled for his son. His wife was terrified but was holding it together. Then Gabe's heart went to his knees, along with his stomach to the floor.

"You and you," he pointed at Lucy and Hannah, "come with us."

"No." Gabriel snapped, reaching for his gun.

The taller ordered the shorter to hold the gun on him. The shorter did as he, or she, was told. Gabe gasped as something stung him in the ribs. Had he been shot? It only took him a moment to realize he had been shot with a drug, not a bullet. He could only pray it was just a knockout drug that wouldn't affect his breathing. He had to protect his family and the others, but he had to sleep. He fell into darkness before he could do anything about it.

* * * * *

Lucy saw her husband fall. "You killed him," she blurted.

"No, just put him to sleep for a bit, same as the other officers. Now, leave the kid, get the girl, and let's go."

Lucy slid Kallie into the arms of her brother, Matthew, and took Hannah's hand. She took one last look at her husband and the other two men lying on the floor and mouthed I love you to her kids. She and Hannah followed the men out the window, and that was the last thing she remembered.

* * * * *

I clutched my son. *They were gone, right? But they had Lucy and Hannah. We had to get out of here.* It was then I realized I hadn't heard the roar of an engine. I gulped. *What if?* Just then, I saw a figure approaching from the room again. The person held out their arms. "Oh, dear God, not my baby. If he goes, you take me too."

"And me." Brad gripped my arm.

"No, he said I could only get the baby. I'll do my best to protect him. I'm a hostage too."

"Get out here, or I'll shoot you," the voice yelled.

"Give me the baby," she yelped and grabbed my son. I'd already lost Emily. I panicked.

* * * * *

Gabe could feel himself coming around. Whatever he'd been given wasn't strong. "Thank You, God!" He might have a chance at catching them. Gabe heard the two officers on the floor next to him stir. He stood but fell on his back side. Cam and Mark raced to their dad's side. Gabe noticed Kallie in Matt's arms. It was at that minute he heard the roar of a vehicle starting.

"Aaron, get a description and direction of travel on it, son, please."

"They have Mom, sis, and the baby."

It wasn't until then he noticed the baby missing from Alex's arms.

"No," he groaned. "Let's go after them," he said as he and the other officers raced for the door. "Stay here, and here is a burner phone. Call if you hear any sound at all."

"I'll stay with them," Officer Kenton said. "Someone should be here."

Not that it did much good apparently and not that Gabe would voice that out loud.

"Okay, let's go."

Was every road in the smokies this curvy? Probably, Gabe had grown up here and knew a lot of them well. But the drug was still messing with his stomach. With the car in their sights, they radioed the plate and their situation. Backup was on the way, but could they get there in time? The officer who was driving had a wave of nausea hit and had to stop. That cost them precious seconds they didn't have, and they lost sight of them.

"Dear God, please keep them safe."

"We need a chopper in the air," Gabe yelled in the radio. "We lost sight of them."

"Already on it." Their chief came back calm but shaken. "We have units at all points where they could come out."

Unless they went off road, Gabe thought to himself.

They all knew the possibility, and that would make for a harder search, however not impossible. God was still in control, not the crooks.

* * * * *

I told the officer who had stayed behind with us what the woman had said when she snatched my son. He gasped and got on his radio. I fell into Brad's arms and fell apart. Both our kids were now missing, and I couldn't survive if they didn't.

"Let's pray."

That came from little Kallie in Matt's arms. I pulled back and reached out my arms for the child. "That sounds like the best idea I've heard all day."

Chapter 13

With all hands on board, the hunt was on. It was now even more personal. They had his wife and daughter. Now, they had taken Brad and Alex's new baby. Thankfully, if they let them stay together, Lucy would care for him. *If they…no, not going there.*

"Please, dear God, let them be alive." Just as he finished his prayer, the radio crackled with information. The officer from the house was saying something. Gabriel strained to focus.

"The second one, the woman with him, is a hostage. She needs help."

They all did. God was the only one who could perform that miracle.

* * * * *

Lucy gagged and opened her eyes. She took inventory of her surroundings. It was a building, possibly metal, and it was kind of cold, no, really cold, like maybe they were underground. No, that wouldn't make sense, but then again, maybe so. She went to scrub a hand through her hair and then realized she was zip-tied. She tried to think. Somehow, she had to get free. She kicked her feet. Someone had messed up. They had left her feet undone.

It was pitch-black in the shed, so the only looking around to do was with your hands, your feet, and your other senses. She took a deep breath. She smelled, what, fresh dirt. Okay, maybe they were underground, but, unless they had done some fancy work, not buried.

Lucy took a moment to pray. She needed and wanted God to lead her. She used her fingers to feel around, she might be zip-tied, but her fingers somehow still moved. That had to be God. She pushed to her feet, feeling her stomach lurch. "No, no, not now, please, God, we have to get out of here." She continued praying silently as she started searching.

First, she found her daughter Hannah. She then found another much smaller body. *Emily? But where was the baby, and was this Emily?*

"Please, dear God! No."

She couldn't find a pulse in the little girl. She felt the child's long braids. She then moved back to her own daughter. Hanna's pulse was faint. She had to get these restraints off. She began moving her hands one way and then another. Whoever had zip-tied her hadn't meant for them to stay on but to appear that way—strange. She dropped them and knelt next to her daughter.

"Hannah, Hannah," she said in one breath, "wake up. We've got to get out of here. Come on, sweet girl. You can do this."

Hannah moaned, and Lucy felt her roll her head one way and then the other. She clasped Hannah's hands to find them zip-tied. Hannah's feet were too, but it only took Lucy seconds to free her frightened daughter.

"Come on." She didn't dare mention the deceased girl in the corner. She led Hannah, using the wall as a guide.

"Mom, I can't see."

"Me either, Hannah. Just bear with me, and pray with everything in you."

* * * * *

Gabriel was sick with worry. It had been five hours and no sign of his wife, daughter, or Brad and Alex's baby. He smacked himself in the forehead and then wondered why. Then, in the bedroom of the safe house that he had shared with his wife only hours ago, he hit his knees.

He and Lucy had always been able to read one another, even from a distance apart. Like that time he was at training and he had sensed she was afraid. She had been home with their young son and heard a strange noise outdoors. He'd called, and she told him she had been about to call. He hung up and called a buddy who had been on duty. It turned out to just be some kids trampling through the yard, but still, he knew now that she was in trouble, and not only because he knew the facts. God had put them together, and death would be the only thing to separate them, and he prayed that would be a while yet.

His kids joined him, and he invited Brad to join them. He agreed. They all prayed, even the officers from their watch points outside the house.

* * * * *

Lucy could feel her husband praying. She half expected to half to kick her way out. The flimsy door didn't give her much of a challenge. However, once it fell open, she gasped. "Dear God, now what are we supposed to do?" Lucy wanted to sit right down and cry. But she couldn't do that. Suddenly, a noise sent her nerves more on edge, if that were possible.

"Hide," she whispered.

Together, they slid back inside the metal building and held up the door. It was poorly lit inside the cellar, so they wouldn't notice.

"Get in there. You've caused me nothing but trouble, and you can die with the rest of them."

Then there was a scream, along with a slamming door.

"Here, take this screaming brat of a baby."

After the door closed a second time, Lucy ventured from her hiding spot. She told Hannah to stay put until she checked things out. When she saw the figure, she recognized her, at least the outline.

"It's all right, I won't hurt you. He will though."

Hannah slid out beside her, and they let the door fall.

"Who are you?" Lucy asked.

"You can call me Jade. My name is Corah Jade Keansten."

Over the next hour, the young woman told Lucy how he had kept her captured the last ten years. She explained each time he had gotten her pregnant, he had made her leave the babies in various locations.

"Except the one I lost, poor baby, but at least he or she is in heaven out of this mess."

She's a believer, Lucy thought.

"I took care of this little one and Emily the best I could. But one night, he knocked me out and took Emily out of the house."

"Took her?" Lucy was sick in heart and body.

"The night he made me help kidnap Emily from her home, I didn't want too. I did as he said because I knew he'd kill me. I watched him hit Emily's dad, and I picked up Emily. He always makes me get the kids. Then I saw a bag with her name on it on the counter. There was a light on in the kitchen."

"Her medicine?" Lucy whispered, "You—" Lucy let her thoughts trail off.

"Yea, I'm her biological mother. I wanted to keep her alive. I wanted her to go home to her parents. It was never supposed to be this way."

"He had you put her at dispatch knowing Versie was working, didn't he?"

"Yea, he did." Tears choked her voice. "You have no idea how bad I wanted to run in there and ask for help. But he would have shot me and them. Anyone who would have tried to help me. He kept track of her, Versie."

"Where did he have you leave the other baby?" Lucy was starting to untangle the cobwebs in her head.

"Umm, it's hard to relive."

"You don't have to. You can just tell the cops when we are found." They would be found, if she was still carrying that air tag in her coat pocket, which she was. *Wait, oh no.*

* * * * *

Something occurred to Gabriel for the first time. Lucy had stuck something in her coat pocket the other night, intending to give it to their daughter. He had already attached it to his phone. If he still had his phone.

"What are you thinking, Isaiah?" the tall deputy sitting next to him asked.

"If we still had my phone and Lucy still had that thing in her pocket, we could track them. But I ditched my phone along with everyone else."

"I know where they are."

"Excuse me?" Gabriel felt a flicker of something—hope!

"Yea, man, they are at the station. Do you think he left her pockets alone?"

Jeffry was tall, black, and Southern. He was a good friend and a good deputy. Gabriel would have him on his side any day.

"We can pray."

"Right on that," Jeffery said, picking up his burner phone to call the station.

Chapter 14

"No," Jade said, handing Lucy the baby, "I'll tell you. That way if—"
She didn't have to finish; Lucy knew.

"He made me leave the other baby with his aunt in California.
Of course, she just found a baby on her front porch."

"Was she one of the women who died?"

"Probably."

Lucy gathered her courage. "We have to get out of here."

"Is that door locked?" Hannah asked. "Probably but—"

Jade reached for the knob. "It's worth a try. But if it is, we will
have to run for it. I don't know this place since I'm not allowed out
of the house, unless he takes me with him on some errand." It turned
and then opened. "Run," Jade said.

They all took out down some path. It was their only hope
though. Jade was in front and then Hannah and then Lucy and the
baby. Lucy heard footsteps behind her.

"Please, God, no. Hannah, take the baby, and run with Jade."
Reluctantly, Hannah obeyed. Lucy turned to face her captor. She
squared her shoulders and felt a strength that wasn't her own. He
stopped.

"Aren't you going to run with the rest of them, or do you think
you will keep my attention off them?"

Lucy gulped.

"Well, little lady, there are cameras all over this place. I thought
I might mess up one of these days, and looks like I did." He sighed
and grabbed her hand. She flinched. At least he hadn't zip-tied her

again. She had a feeling he hadn't been the one to do it. If he had, they wouldn't be loose right now. She prayed Hannah, the baby, and Jade would find safety. Then, she prayed for her own safety. She really wanted to go home.

* * * * *

Gabriel nearly had a coronary when his friend and fellow officer told him who had been on the other end of the burner phone he kept stashed for the moment. The man had gray eyes and hair slowly growing to match. He was tall but was a teddy bear. He loved Gabe and Lucy's kids, and they loved him. At the moment, Kallie Ann sat on his lap.

"Well," he took a deep breath and shifted the toddler, "the hostage and your daughter made it to a gas station, with Brad and Alex's baby. I need to go tell them."

"May I?" Gabe stood.

The man nodded his approval. "Also, another unit is bringing them here. Other units will make sure they aren't followed."

He couldn't wait to hug his daughter and, after Alex and Brad, snuggle the little guy. His heart broke for the other hostage, Jade. *How long had she been a hostage?* She'd give her statement, and he would read the documents later. For now, they were safe, and where was Lucy?

"Dear God, protect my wife. We need her, Lord."

He found Brad and Alex on the sofa talking to his kids.

"We have some good," he stopped, "and some bad news. The good first, of course. Brad, Alex, your son is safe. Kids, your sister Hannah is safe. They got away because of the mercy and everlasting grace of God. Your mother turned to face the man after telling them to take the baby and run. She's missing. Alex—" He broke off.

"It's bad, isn't it?" she said with a knowing in her eyes.

"Emily is no longer with us." He gave the moment the silence it deserved. No one should have to endure this.

"The hostage admitted to being her biological mother, and the hostage-taker is her sperm donor."

60

Alex hit her knees, and Brad did the same wrapping his arms around her. Gabriel motioned for his kids to follow, to give them some time. They joined the other officer, still holding Kallie Ann and trying to gather himself.

"That little girl didn't deserve to die."

"No, she didn't." Gabe's heart broke as if she would have been one of his own. And it easily could have been Hannah Faith. Just then, the door opened, with a key. Hannah ran straight into her daddy's arms. The brothers surrounded their sister. God does answer prayers, every day, every moment.

* * * * *

Lucy could barely keep up, trying to keep him from dragging her.

"Get in the car."

Where was he taking her? A thought hit her and then an idea. "Can I use your restroom first?" The last place she wanted to go was in that house, but if he searched her pockets, he'd find the air tag.

"Real quick, and nothing funny."

There was no window in the stinky restroom. The shower was nasty and, if possible, the toilet worse. She transferred the tag to her shoe, inside of her sock, flushed the toilet, and washed her hands in a surprisingly clean sink. *What was this?* She hurried out of the bathroom. Once in the car, she headed for the passenger door.

"You really think I'd let you ride up front?"

She had a feeling he wouldn't, but she had to try. "Maybe. I, uh, don't like tight places," she blurted.

"Good." He grinned a rude and rather creepy grin. "All the more reason to put you there."

Why had she said that? Urgh. With that, everything went black.

* * * * *

Gabe listened to Jade share with Alex everything, every gruesome detail. After the first five minutes, he knew they needed a recorder. With Jade aware it was happening, the other officer, Ronny, had her start over and recorded everything. It was better than her writing it all out later.

"He made me leave another baby with his aunt Charlote, in California. The day I left Emily at dispatch, you don't know how bad I wanted to run in and yell help. He would have shot me or anyone else in his way though. I was there when he took Emily from you all. He had watched Versie from the moment he made me leave Emily there. He let me buy one blanket before I gave birth to her, unassisted. The night he took her, made me grab her, I made a vow to myself. I would do whatever it took to keep her alive."

"That's why you took the medicine." Alex put a shaky arm around the trembling young woman.

"I tried, I really did. But he wouldn't let me take care of her of course. He didn't want her, and I wasn't supposed to either. He would never let me out of sight to run away. If he did, I was tied, so I couldn't get away. He just messed up, in our favor today."

* * * * *

Lucy felt groggy. Something else, but what was it? Sick? Yes, that was it. She felt sick, but why? Where was she at anyway? Then it hit her in a blur. She was locked in a trunk. She didn't know where she was, but panic would get her nowhere. She took some deep breaths, in through her nose and out through her mouth. Then, she prayed, really hard.

She took stock of her situation. The car was turned off, and it wasn't moving. She could hear music and, occasionally, other people talking. Were they in a parking lot? Next time she heard people, she would beat on the inside of the trunk.

She pushed on the back of the seat. It wouldn't budge. She found the taillight and kicked with all she had in her. It busted on the cement on her third try. That should get attention. As soon as she heard female voices, she screamed.

"Get help," someone said. "There is someone in that trunk."

Thank You, Lord! Now, she might have a fighting chance.

* * * * *

Gabe's friend's radio crackled to life. "Dispatch to all units." She paused. "All units, respond to Buffey's Bar parking lot. There is a woman locked in a trunk. She has kicked out the taillight and screamed. My caller has left the scene."

They'd want to question the caller, but he didn't blame them.

"Did you get contact information?" an officer requested.

"10-4. Address and telephone number. Be advised, the vehicle is a red car. The caller couldn't give a model. The plate is 555MJF. 555 Mary John Frank. It is stolen."

Of course, it was. Gabriel wanted to be out there. John Hancock jumped to his feet. "Gotta go, boys." He headed to the door.

"Let me go with you," Gabriel pleaded. "That could be my wife. I'd like to be there for her."

"Let me clear it with the chief."

Actually, it's the assistant chief. Their chief was still in the hospital from a gunshot wound this guy caused him.

"I have the okay. Let's go."

Gabe hesitated. "Man, don't leave my kids."

They had been friends for ten years. He knew he could trust the man, still holding his daughter, not to leave his kids.

Hannah and the other kids had understood why he was leaving, but they were scared. Alex had Hannah wrapped in a bear hug at the moment, so that helped. But it wasn't her mother.

They sped down Main and onto Fifth and then into one of the worst places in town. A group had gathered around the car, and officers were shooing them away like flies. This was ridiculous. Why hadn't they gotten her out yet? He prayed for patience and for comfort for he and Lucy and the kids.

Then, what no one saw coming happened. A man who Gabe would recognize anywhere came bursting out of the bar, obviously drunk. He threw himself into the driver's seat.

"Get back," someone yelled.

The person trying to open the trunk barely got out of the way in time. He threw the car in reverse, and every unit on scene gave chase.

"Dear God, no, no, no. No!"

* * * * *

Lucy kicked at the trunk, but it was no use. She now let herself melt into tears. She started crying out to God as loud as she could. Then, a peace came over her that could have only come from God above and of her heart. She started singing. Every gospel song she could think of, she sang. It felt like they were going one hundred miles per hour, but probably not. Behind them, she could hear the sirens. Her husband was probably among them. In between every song, a scripture flashed across her heart. Was their children safe? "Dear God, get me out of here alive. Please, my children need me."

The thought occurred to her that Gabe could take care of them if something happened to her. But that would never do. She kicked out the other taillight and started to kick about where the latch should be.

* * * * *

Gabe had heard her screaming as the car lurched backward. He knew that was Lucy, his only love, his wife and best friend in this world, and the mother of his children. "They'd best not ram him." He choked out. "She's in there."

"No. You and I know they will have to use another tactic."

Gabe knew that as he watched John skillfully maneuver the patrol cruiser and gaped. "Dear God, let him keep it on the road. Stop him, God."

The man had nearly gone off a large drop-off, and that would have most likely killed anyone inside the car. His stomach churned, and he closed his eyes briefly.

"They're putting out spike strips ahead. I hope he runs out of gas or something."

Just then, the man hit the strip. Gabe's friend, driving the car he was riding in, missed it by inches. A few miles later, on fumes, the car came to a halt in the intersection. The guy jumped out, gun in hand. He ran. Thankfully, the intersection was blocked off, so the car couldn't be hit. Gabriel jumped out of the patrol car and headed for the red one, as ten other units gave chase on foot after the man. His minutes of freedom were numbered. At least Gabriel prayed so.

* * * * *

Lucy's head was spinning. She was going to be sick. She had to get out of here. She heard voices and someone working to get the trunk open. She also smelled gas. They must have smelled it too because she heard them instruct dispatch to send the fire department.

As soon as it popped open, Lucy sprang out, only to lose her balance and tumble to the ground. Strong arms, which she knew very well, picked her up and folded her into a bear hug.

"I thought I'd never see you again."

"Until heaven, I know."

"I love you, Luc."

"I love you, Gabe. Where is our children?"

"Safe." He kissed her lips in a tender slow but quick kiss. "Now, let's get you to the hospital."

She was put into a waiting ambulance, and Gabe climbed in beside her. Once at the hospital and she was medically cleared, detectives got her statement. She hung on until the part about finding Emily. They waited patiently while Gabe held her and let her cry. He let go of her hand, which he had been holding since the first minutes in the ambulance and held her against him.

"Let it out, Luc, let it out."

She did. For the next ten minutes, they just cried and thanked the Lord above. They also prayed the man would be caught; he was still on the run. It'd been a pretty thick patch of woods he had run into. Cops lost sight of him. They were searching, but he was nowhere to be found.

Their kids, Jade, Alex, Brad, and the baby joined them at the hospital. Hannah had a fractured wrist. The baby miraculously checked out well. Jade was badly undernourished. She would need a place to stay, and Alex and Brad had already made up their minds where that would be.

Jade had been a foster child. When she had turned eighteen, she had had no one. Her foster family hadn't been those to take her in as their own. So now, she would have found herself alone again. They had all lost Emily. This was her biological mother, and she and Alex already shared a bond so deep. Lucy held each of her kids close. Lucy had some fractured ribs and a headache that would subside. Being tossed around in a trunk at ninety-five miles an hour really didn't leave many places not sore. Gabe had told her the real speed.

As he held her and talked to their children, he kept an eye on the window. He was listening closely to what their children were saying, but she could tell he had saw something he wasn't liking.

"What is it?" she whispered. "You aren't going anywhere are you?"

"Not right now." For the next ten minutes, he just watched.

"I saw his sedan down there, Lucy. It was him."

"Gabe, we are four stories up. Are you sure?"

"Yea, no question."

She watched Gabe talking to another officer, nod, and then walk over to her.

"They have got officers on every door of this place, the exits anyway. We are going down to talk to security. You have security on your door." He kissed her lips. "So keep the kids in here with you. Alex, Brad, and the baby are in with Jade. They have the same. I'll be back soon. I love you. Most of all, God is with us."

"Love you, Dad," came from around the room.

"I love you too. Please, honey, be careful. Do you have to go?" Lucy was used to this, yet the tears dripped down her face. "I know you do."

"I love all of you. I need, want, to see what's going on. They must have some suspicion he's coming here." Sure, the others would keep him posted, but Gabriel needed, wanted, to be involved in catching this guy. He hadn't mentioned anything to anyone, except Lucy and the other officer, about seeing the sedan. Since they were covering the hospital, he hadn't had to. When they got down to the others, he might. He could be wrong. Lucy was right; they were a pretty good ways up.

Chapter 15

I hadn't let go of my baby, except for letting Brad and Gabriel hold him, since I got him back in my arms. Emily was gone. She was in heaven with Jesus and Mom, but gone from my sight. I lost my battle with the tears I'd been fighting back since my first breakdown.

The overly amazing joy that my son was back in our arms and safe was incredible. I wasn't going to discount that fact, but Emily was gone. She was supposed to smile when she saw the baby. She liked to feel him when he was moving and kicking in my stomach. She would have been the sweetest big sister, but now, she'd never get the chance. What was it with some people? Why could they ever become parents? They weren't parents. But it wasn't my place to question God, and I didn't really want too. It wasn't fair that we had lost Emily at the hands of her biological dad no less. No, it wasn't. But the precious girl would never have to suffer a seizure, test, or illness again.

"Thank you, dear sweet Jesus," I whispered in Brad's arms. This truth was all that was getting me through, as I knew Emily was being taken for an autopsy at the morgue. Gabe walked alongside several other officers. Surely, the guy wouldn't come here. The place was hopping with units, and if he showed up, he was going down, but maybe he would.

Five minutes later, they were in front of the hospital emergency entrance, talking with other officers. Two other detectives, Mark and Robert, stood there, looking at Gabe.

"What are you doing out here? You should be up there with your wife and kids in protection."

"Give him a break," Robert said. "You know how it is. He's one of us."

"I do." The man gave Gabe a sheepish half grin.

Unfortunately, the man knew all too well what this was. Most of them did. The man was just looking out for him. He knew that and would thank him later.

"Any update on this suspect?" Gabe wanted to call him a perp but refrained.

"He was spotted running through a backyard that joins the field, which joins the woods he ran out of. That was about twenty minutes ago."

Just as Gabriel began to share what he saw, out the window on the other side of the building, a silver sedan wheeled up in front of them and stopped with a screech. Immediately, everyone recognized its male driver and the car. Gabe started praying for a miracle because they were going to need one. He closed his eyes for a moment and prayed God would give them guidance. *He* hadn't left them this far, and *He* certainly wouldn't now. God was the only one who knew the right moves and the outcome of this. It pays to listen to *Him*. Gabe looked at their assistant chief, Ronny.

"Here is the plan." The man gave it five in seconds.

* * * * *

From her place in the bed upstairs, Lucy wondered what had happened to Gabe. He'd been gone a while, and she and the kids were getting nervous. The guards outside the door couldn't tell Matthew anything when he had asked.

"Dear God, please keep my husband safe."

* * * * *

Gabe watched the man he had questioned only weeks ago step from the car. He wore a mask, but it didn't do much for him. Gabe recognized his build. He looked at his chief for clearance, and he gave it. "Take the mask off, Marcum, it isn't helping you."

"Recognize me do you, detective? Don't stand in my way, and no one gets hurt."

The guards covering the front doors of the emergency room never wavered. Neither did Gabe nor any of the others. Marcum pulled off the mask and threw it on the ground. That would need to be bagged for evidence. He slid his gun from his side, and Gabe and the others held theirs steady.

"Come on, Marcum," Gabe said. "Let's do this the easy way. We don't want anyone hurt, including you."

"Where is Jade? She needs to be with me. She's involved too, with me, you know."

"Oh, we know," Gabe said.

"Then, where is she? Where is Jade?"

"That's not information we can divulge," Gabe's superior spoke up.

The man was getting impatient, and his gun pointed straight at Gabriel. "Do you want to see your family again, detective?"

"You know I do." Gabe kept his voice even and measured. "Put that gun down, Marcum. Let's talk."

"I'm done talking. I'm going to start shooting." He swung the gun off Gabriel and toward the guards covering the doors. Even though the hospital was on lockdown and doors would only open if done so from inside, one bullet would gain him access to the whole building. The guards pointed their weapons right back and flinched when a bullet wiped passed them and ended up in the building's exterior. "That was a warning. Next time, I'll be serious."

Next time he would be serious? What did that mean? How much more serious could you get?

The man turned and then turned back to the doors and the guards. When the man wasn't looking, Timmy took up his position. One wrong move and Marcum would have a bullet in his back.

* * * * *

Matthew was getting desperate. His dad had been gone a long time. He paced the floor and then went to stand beside his mother. "Where is dad?" he whispered.

"I don't know, but I sure wish they would tell us something."

Matt tried again. He stepped to the door and cracked it open. "Is my dad all right?"

"I'll tell you when I can. He is alive."

That was good to know.

"He's helping with something, Matt," the other guard explained. "He will be back when he can."

"Thanks, Rodgers."

Matt closed the door and went to tell his mother. They both knew that meant he was helping with security.

* * * * *

Gabe breathed a constant prayer. He did want to return to his family. This guy was crazy and didn't care who he hurt. Gabe watched Marcum and then stole a glance at Timmy. He was watching the man like a hawk, and Gabe knew the man really didn't want to use his gun, unless that was the only resource left. Gabe took another try with the man. "Marcum, what are you gaining from this?"

"Well, hopefully, my freedom. What do you think?"

"Well, this isn't getting you any closer. If you shoot an officer, it's going to get you more time."

Or shot, but Gabe left that part silent. He watched decision work on the man's face.

"I don't care." He raised his gun.

"Marcum, don't do this."

One shot rang out and then two. Marcum lay on the ground, and so did one of the officers guarding the door. Instantly, someone kicked the gun out of the man's reach. Medical personnel were summoned, and the injured were put on beds. Gabe followed his injured officer friend to the ER doors.

"I need to go let Lucy and the kids know I'm fine," he told the assistant chief.

"Go ahead. I'll keep you updated. Good job out there, Isaiah. You sure you're ready to retire?"

"Beyond ready, now."

* * * * *

As soon as Gabe entered the room, Lucy held out her arms. "What happened? You have blood on you."

"Are you hurt?" Hannah asked with a squeal in her voice.

"No, honey. Some others were. Pray for them. In fact, let's pray now." Gabe led them in a prayer of thanksgiving and then for protection for the injured. He prayed that Marcum would give his heart to God before it was too late and that his officer buddy would pull through. "It's in Jesus's Holy Name we pray, amen."

Kallie had said the word *Amen* along with him. It brought a much-needed smile to his face.

"Now," Gabe stood letting go of his wife's hand, "I have a young lady to tell after ten years she is safe."

"Amen," Lucy praised God with everything in her for that and more.

Chapter 16

My heart broke for Jade and everything she had been through. We were trying to share all the good stories with her about Emily that we could. There would Lord-willing be much time for more stories and lots of pictures. She also wanted to know about her daughter's (because Emily was her daughter) medical history. We explained the best we could and then just all took a moment to bask in the fact that she was with Jesus and no longer suffering.

At that quiet minute, a knock on the door came. Brad told whoever it was to come in. We knew the hospital was on lockdown and we had guards on our door, so we were safe.

Detective Gabriel Isaiah stood in the doorway, a mixed expression covering his face.

"Detective?" I asked. "Is everything okay?" That was a crazy way to put it.

"Alex," he came in and shut the door, "as much as we've all been through together lately, Lucy and I consider you all family. Just call me Gabe, you too Brad and Jade. Jade, I've got some good news, for all of you really."

We all waited, expecting what?

"Okay." Jade's ocean-blue eyes were on him, her complete attention waiting to know what it was he felt was good news.

"You are free. Your captor is not."

"What are you saying?" She was processing.

"Jade," Gabe walked closer, "he came to the hospital and tried shooting his way inside. He shot one of our guys. He is in surgery now. But he also took a bullet, and he's going to be all right. But he is in custody. He's going away for a long time. You are safe."

"Thank You, God." The young woman covered her face and wept with pure thanksgiving unto God. "I'll have to face him in court, won't I?" She let her hands fall on her lap, but her expression of peace never wavered.

"Yes." Gabe wasn't going to fib to the young woman. She was going to have to see him in court. But, thankfully, the man who had held her captive for so long would be in shackles and cuffs.

"With God, nothing shall be impossible." She breathed. "That's the scripture I clung to for ten years and six months. Without Him, I wouldn't be here."

That was an Amazing God testimony to hear from someone who had just survived what she did. Gabe was honored to have been there to have heard it and to tell her she was safe from the creep—poor girl knew down to how many months she had been held captive.

* * * * *

After Lucy had been released from the hospital, the Isaiahs were driven home. The officers who took them were kind enough to let the family stop and grab some food and coffee. They all were blessed to be alive, and they none discounted that fact. Even little Kallie Ann jumped for joy when they entered the house and screamed, "Thank You, Jesus!"

They all joined her, receiving a few looks from the neighbors, as the front door still remained open. No one cared. Lucy and Gabe shouted, "Hallelujah, dear sweet Jesus! You've done it again."

They stood on their front porch but really wished they could have shouted it from the rooftop.

"Now, let's get everyone ready for bed," Lucy said.

"I'm right behind you, dear, right behind you.

"You go put on a pot of coffee, and I'll get the kids in bed. I need to process."

He headed to the kitchen to do just that.

Chapter 17

The next morning, we woke up in our own house and our own bed. I could fix scrambled eggs in my own kitchen instead of a safe house.

It was really starting to hit me that we had lost Emily and could have lost our son. I kissed him and held him a little tighter as I fed him. Jade was still in the hospital and would be for a few days. My husband was fixing her a room up, a room that still should have been the room we used for Emily's things: her extra wheelchair, for when we took her on trails, which she loved, and her machine we used when we needed to suction her. I couldn't think about the rest of the things: her clothes, the few toys she actually paid attention to, and the stuffed police bear Gabe had given her still lying on her little bed in our bedroom. I picked it up, after I had laid the baby down, and raised it to my face. Emily's scent was all over it. I let myself fall into a puddle of tears and didn't even try to stop them.

Brad came out of the shower at that moment and embraced me in a hug. I let him hold me against him. I needed him, and he needed me. Mark 10:9 would hold true forever and always. It is true. You do become one when you say I do, and without God in there, I don't know how people survive. We couldn't. We just stayed that way for the next hour, holding each other, praying, and clinging to God's Word and His everlasting promises. Court would come soon enough, and I would need all God's strength He would bless me with.

Gabe received word when the court proceedings would begin. He was ready, and then he wasn't. This was personal. His heart broke for Lucy; she was going to have to see her cousin's murderer. Not that she hadn't seen him before, but that fact would make it hard on her too. She still woke them up with a nightmare that she was trapped in a trunk. But the mix of finding Emily in that dark prison mixed and mingled unwelcomed with that nightmare. In her nightmare of the trunk, she was trapped with a dead body, Emily's dead body.

Jade had tried keeping the girl alive; she had wanted to help her daughter so badly. But the man had knocked her out and taken Emily out. It would be a no-brainer as far as conviction went, on all counts. Gabe glared at the calendar. Two weeks now remained until his day of retirement. He was ready for it now.

Note from Samantha

Well, what did you think? It was hard writing the loss of Emily. The loss of any loved one is rough, but the loss of a child has its own category.

I pray this book has been a blessing to you. Please let us know by reviewing this book on Amazon or Goodreads, or let us know on Facebook. Follow @God's Silver Lining.

I hope you like Detective Isaiah and his family. Lord-willing, there will be a series featuring these kind fictional folks. Stay tuned to our Facebook page, and follow me on Amazon for updates.

I'm so grateful to God Almighty for blessing me to go on this journey of writing. Also, I'm grateful to my family and friends who pray for and support me and also to Momma's fur baby daughter, Mommy loves you, Ashton Nicole. Thanks to my grandmothers who read every book. I love you both.

God just keeps on blessing me.

> For we walk by faith, not by sight. (2 Corinthians 5:7 KJV)

Amen. *Praise His holy name.*

About the Author

Samantha was born and grew up in Kentucky. Having optic nerve hypoplasia has brought its challenges, but with God granting peace, Samantha has accepted her visual struggles. Samantha is a dog mom, an auntie, and a singer. She is grateful for the family and friends who support her and is always reading the Bible or a good Christian fiction suspense or romance. Laura Scott, Lynette Eason, and Karen Kingsbury are three of Samantha's inspirational authors.